To Millie + Evie Wood.

For being good.

MERRY CHRISTMAS!

From Santa

Santa is coming to Bradford

Written by Steve Smallman
Illustrated by Robert Dunn and Jerry Pyke
Designed by Sarah Allen

First published by Hometown World in 2012
Hometown World Ltd
7 Northumberland Buildings
Bath BA1 2JB

www.hometownworld.co.uk

Copyright © Hometown World Ltd 2012

ISBN 978-1-84993-301-8
Printed in China

Santa is coming to Bradford

Written by Steve Smallman  Illustrated by Robert Dunn

DISCOVER MORE OF YOUR TOWN
HOMETOWN WORLD

"Well?"

boomed Santa. "Have all the children from **Bradford** been good this year?"

"Well...erm...mostly," answered the little old elf, as he bustled across the busy workshop to Santa's desk.

Santa peered down at the elf from behind the tall, teetering piles of letters that the children of Bradford had sent him.

"Mostly?" asked Santa,
looking over the top of his glasses.

"Yes...but they've all been **especially** good in the last few days!" said the elf.

"Jolly good!" chuckled Santa.
"Then we'd better get their presents loaded up!"

Even though the sack of presents was

really, really big

and the elves were really, really small,

they seemed to have no trouble loading it onto Santa's sleigh.
Though how they managed to fit such a big sack into one little sleigh
even they didn't know. But somehow they did.

"Splendid!" boomed Santa. "We're ready to go!"

"Er...not quite, Santa," said the little old elf. "One of our reindeer is missing!"

"Missing?

Which reindeer is missing?" asked Santa.

"The youngest one, Santa," said the elf. "It's his first flight tonight. I've called him and called him, but..."

Just then, a young reindeer strolled up, munching on a large carrot.

"where have you been?"

asked Santa.

But the youngest reindeer was crunching so loudly that it was no wonder he hadn't heard the little old elf calling.

"Oh well, never mind," said Santa, giving the reindeer a little wink. He took out his Santa-nav and tapped in the postcode BD1 for Bradford. **"This will guide us to Bradford in no time."**

Crunch! Crunch! Crunch!

With a flick of the reins and a jerk of the harness, off they went, racing through the sky.

"Ho-ho-ho!"

laughed Santa.

"We'll soon have these parcels
delivered to Wool City!"

Santa's sleigh flew through the starry night heading south across the North Sea. On they flew in the crisp, wintry air, crossing the coast above Hartlepool. In the wink of an eye, the sleigh was flying above Ripon on the right and Otley on the left. The youngest reindeer was very excited. He had never been away from the North Pole before.

They were just crossing the Chevin
when, suddenly, they ran into a blizzard.
Snowflakes whirled around the sleigh.

They couldn't see a thing!

The youngest reindeer was getting a bit worried,
But Santa didn't seem worried.

"In two kilometres..."

said the Santa-nav in a bossy lady's voice,

"...keep left at the next star."

"But, Madam," Santa blustered, "I can't see any stars in all this snow!"

Soon they were

hopelessly lost!

Bong-bong!
Bong-bong!

Then, through the howling blizzard, the youngest reindeer heard a faint, ringing sound.

Bong-bong!

He looked over at the old reindeer with the red nose. But he had his head down.

(Red nose...I wonder who that could be?)

Bong-bong!
Bong-bong!

Bong-bong!
Bong-bong!

There was that sound
again, like clock chimes
ringing. The youngest
reindeer turned round to look
at Santa. But Santa wasn't
listening. He seemed to be
arguing with a little box
with buttons on it.

With a flick of the
harness and a jerk of the
reins, the youngest reindeer gave a
sharp *tug* and headed off towards
the sound of the chimes, pulling Santa
and his sleigh behind him!

"Whoa!"

cried Santa, pulling his hat straight.
"What's going on?" Then, to his surprise,
he heard a ringing sound.

"Well done, young reindeer!" he shouted
cheerfully. "It must be Bradford Cathedral.
Don't worry, children, Santa is coming!"

But, suddenly...

CRUNCH!

The sleigh hit something as it plummeted through the snow clouds. **"YOU HAVE ARRIVED!"** said the Santa-nav unhelpfully.

Finally, when the snow had died down and the clouds parted, Santa discovered exactly where they were...

...stuck, right around the top of the
City Hall clock tower!

"Everybody, PULL!"

The reindeer *pulled* with all their might until, at last, with a screeching noise, the sleigh scraped clear of the tower and Santa steered them safely over Bradford Cathedral, past St George's Hall, across the railway line and down into Bowling Park.

Luckily, there
was no real
damage done, but
the parcels had all
been jumbled up. Santa
quickly sorted out the
presents into order again.

"Right," said Santa. "Thanks to
this young reindeer I know where
we are now. Don't worry, children,

Santa is coming!"

Santa drove his sleigh expertly from rooftop to rooftop all over Bradford, popping in and out of chimneys as fast as he could go.

(Which was pretty fast for a chubby chap!)

There were big chimneys in Daisy Hill, and small chimneys in Eccleshill. He squeezed down thin chimneys in Buttershaw and plummeted down fat chimneys in Idle.

The youngest reindeer was amazed at how quickly they went. Santa never seemed to get tired at all! And it looked like the children in Bradford were going to be very lucky this year! But the youngest reindeer was starting to feel a bit weary and quite hungry too!

In house after house, Santa delved inside his sack for parcels of every shape and size.

He piled them under the Christmas trees and carefully filled up the stockings with surprises.

Santa took a little bite out of each mince pie, a tiny sip of something, wiped his beard and popped the carrots into his sack.

In house after house, the good children of Bradford had left out a large mince pie, a small glass of something and a big, crunchy carrot.

From Four Lane Ends to Five Lane Ends, from
Fagley to Wibsey, from Frizinghall to Tyersal, and
ALL the places in between, Santa and his sleigh
visited every house in Bradford.

Santa delivered presents to Aja, Abi, Ben, Bev, Charlie, Chelsey...the list went on and on! ...Zac, Zara, Zybil.

(Zybil? That must be a spelling mistake, surely!)

Finally, Santa had delivered the last present on his long Bradford list.

"Great moons and stars!" sighed Santa. "It's past midnight and my sack seems as heavy as ever! I hope I haven't forgotten anyone."

Santa opened his sack to check...but it was full of juicy, crunchy carrots!

Santa shared out the carrots between all the reindeer.
"Well done, lad!" he said, patting the youngest reindeer gently on the nose.

But the youngest reindeer didn't hear him...he was too busy munching!

Then it was time to set off for home. Santa reset his Santa-nav once more
to North Pole, and soon they were speeding over Centenary Square
through the crisp, starry night.